MAP of MANITOBA

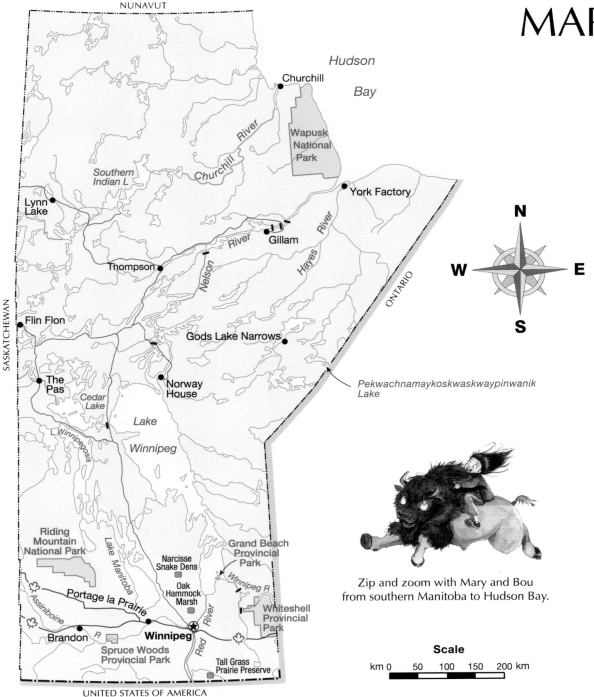

NUNAVUT

Hudson

Bay

Churchill

Wapusk National Park

Churchill River

River

Southern Indian L

Lynn Lake

York Factory

Nelson River

Gillam

Hayes River

Thompson

ONTARIO

SASKATCHEWAN

Flin Flon

Gods Lake Narrows

Pekwachnamaykoskwaskwaypinwanik Lake

The Pas

Norway House

Cedar Lake

Lake Winnipeg

L. Winnipegosis

Lake Manitoba

Riding Mountain National Park

Narcisse Snake Dens

Grand Beach Provincial Park

Winnipeg R

Oak Hammock Marsh

Assiniboine

Whiteshell Provincial Park

Portage la Prairie

Red River

Brandon

R

Winnipeg

Spruce Woods Provincial Park

Tall Grass Prairie Preserve

UNITED STATES OF AMERICA

N
W E
S

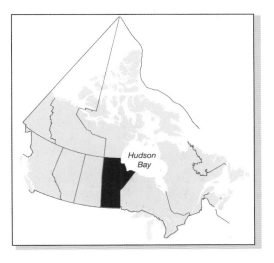

Hudson Bay

Zip and zoom with Mary and Bou
from southern Manitoba to Hudson Bay.

Scale

km 0   50   100   150   200 km

⊛	**Winnipeg – provincial capital**
●	**Other populated places**
—	**Roads**
—✿—	**Trans-Canada Highway**
—·—·—	**International boundary**
—··—··—	**Provincial boundary**
∿	**Hydroelectric dam on a river**
▪	**Other interesting places**
▭	**Boreal forest**

Base map adapted from the Atlas of Canada, Natural Resources Canada.

To learn more about Canada's geography go to www.atlas.gc.ca.

Dedicated to my mom, Mary Melnyk-Muz, and my dad, Leslie Matyas, for introducing me to the joys of reading.

Also dedicated to my husband, Borden Smid, for zipping and zooming with me through life.

– Gwen Smid

To my boys, Timothy and Christian, for being my inspiration.

– Sonia Nadeau

Text copyright © 2008 by Gwen Smid
Illustrations copyright © 2008 by Sonia Nadeau

Second printing 2012
Version française : 2012

Peanut Butter Press
9-1060 Dakota Street,
Winnipeg, MB R2N 1P2
www.peanutbutterpress.ca

This book was typeset with Optima. All illustrations were rendered in watercolour.

Designed by Lisa Rae Swan and Kristin Szuminsky

Printed and bound in Hong Kong at Paramount Printing Company Limited / Book Art Inc., Markham, Ontario, Canada
The hardcover edition of this book is Smyth sewn case bound. The paperback edition of this book is limp bound.

10 9 8 7 6 5 4 3 2

Library and Archive Canada Cataloguing in Publication

Smid, Gwen, 1979-
    Mary's Atlas : Mary Meets Manitoba / Gwen Smid ; Sonia Nadeau, illustrator.
ISBN 978-0-9735579-4-7 (bound).--ISBN 978-0-9735579-3-0 (pbk.)
    1. Manitoba--Juvenile fiction. 2. Manitoba--Juvenile literature. I. Nadeau, Sonia, 1974-
II. Title.
PS8637.M53M37 2008   jC813'.6   C2008-901587-8

Mary's Atlas
Mary Meets Manitoba

By Gwen Smid
Illustrations by Sonia Nadeau

Peanut Butter Press

Mary is in trouble.

Her brother just discovered the slimy gob of worms she put in his shoes. Mary is in her bedroom frantically searching for her atlas. An ordinary atlas is a collection of maps.

This isn't an ordinary atlas.

When Mary taps the cover three times, she can enter any map. She finds her atlas just in time and – tap tap tap – whips it open. The province of Manitoba is staring up at her.

The atlas fizzles and sizzles. It splutters and splatters. It bubbles and pops. Mary shrinks smaller and smaller, tinier and tinier, itsy bitsier and itsy bitsier. In a flurry of sparks and mist, Mary vanishes.

The sparks and mist twirl away. Mary is standing in a large field, atlas in hand.

A little bison is snacking on the tall prairie grass.

"Welcome to Manitoba. My name's Bou." A little dribble rolls down his furry chin. Bou is not a careful eater.

"My name's Mary."

Bou takes another thoughtful mouthful of delicious green grass and nods toward his shaggy back. "Let me show you around."

They zip and zoom over southern Manitoba's fields of yellow canola and blue flax. Farmers are hard at work cutting and baling, their tractors roaring and rumbling over the huge hay fields.

Bou's name comes from "Manitou bou," one of the possible origins of the name "Manitoba." The bison is the provincial animal and one of the symbols on the province's shield, flag, and coat of arms.

"I'll introduce you to the Golden Boy," says Bou. "He stands on top of Manitoba's Legislative Building in Winnipeg. He's a super nice guy."

But the super nice Golden Boy is super duper upset.

The Golden Boy sniffs. "The tricky North Wind stole my torch. If I don't get it back, I can't watch over Manitoba at night."

"We'll find the North Wind!" declares Mary.

The Golden Boy was created in France in 1918. His arrival in Winnipeg was delayed due to World War One.

Mary and Bou swish and swoosh over The Forks Market, located at the junction of the Red and Assiniboine rivers.

"There are lots of fun things to do at The Forks all year round," Bou informs Mary.

The Forks is a National Historic Site of Canada. It was an Aboriginal meeting place, and over time various groups of people have passed through or settled here. Located across the Red River from The Forks is St. Boniface, the largest Francophone community in western Canada.

The tricky North Wind is pestering pedestrians at Portage and Main, Winnipeg's windiest corner. He flaps the flags on the flagpoles. He gusts Granny's groceries out of her hands. He even picks up a pudgy puppy and floats it along like a kite.

"What have you done with the Golden Boy's torch?" Bou demands.

The North Wind howls with laughter. "I blew it into the Red River. If you want to find it, follow the current." Then he disappears.

Winnipeg is Manitoba's capital city. In the Cree language, "Winnipeg" means "muddy waters."

Mary and Bou flip and fly along the Red River until it flows into Lake Winnipeg, Manitoba's largest lake.

Lake Winnipeg, Lake Manitoba, and Lake Winnipegosis are Manitoba's three largest lakes. They are remnants of glacial Lake Agassiz, an ancient lake that once covered much of the province. All water in Manitoba eventually flows north into Hudson Bay because of the slope of the land.

Mary frowns. "I'm sure the water put the torch out. How are we ever going to find it?"

There are more than 100 000 lakes in Manitoba. Most of them are small and located in the northern part of the province. One of these northern Manitoba lakes, Pekwachnamaykoskwaskwaypinwanik Lake, has the longest geographical place name in Canada.

The North Wind returns, whisking the waves into frothy, ferocious peaks. With an extra strong whoosh, he sweeps Mary off Bou's back and she tumbles into the choppy water below.

Mary is sloshed around like juice in a blender.

Something slippery brushes by her icy toes. An enormous sturgeon with nose plugs pops out of the water and helps Mary to shore.

"What's a little girl doing in Lake Winnipeg?" asks the sturgeon.

"What's a fish doing with nose plugs?" asks Mary, curiosity overcoming her chilliness.

The sturgeon grins. "It just so happens that I don't like getting water up my nose."

"Well, it just so happens that we're looking for the Golden Boy's torch!" states Bou. He snuggles up to Mary, his thick brown fur quickly warming her and drying the atlas.

"I saw a torch floating north," the sturgeon says.
They thank him and wave good-bye.

The lake sturgeon of Manitoba were once so plentiful that these large, oily fish were used as fuel for steam-powered boats. Growth rings on the pectoral fin spines of these prehistoric fish show they can live to be around 150 years old.

Mary and Bou sail and swoop over Lake Winnipeg until they reach the Nelson River.

"I've never seen so many pine trees," says Bou. "Where are we?"

Always particularly practical, Mary consults her atlas. "We're in the boreal forest."

"What's that?" Bou asks.

Overhead, an owl, of the great grey variety, clears her throat and fluffs her plumage. "A boreal forest has mainly coniferous trees."

"Coniferous trees?" they both ask, puzzled.

The great grey adjusts her horn-rimmed glasses. "Coniferous trees are trees with cones. Just remember, C is for coniferous and C is for cones."

"Thanks for the info," replies Mary, "but we're looking for a torch."

"I saw a torch floating downstream," the owl hoots.

They thank her and wave good-bye.

The boreal forest covers one-third of Canada. It is known as the lungs of North America because it turns carbon dioxide into oxygen.

The great grey owl is Manitoba's provincial bird. The white spruce is the provincial tree.

They dipsy-doodle north down the Nelson River, where they see huge hydroelectric dams. Generating stations capture the energy of fast-moving water and turn it into electricity so power lines can carry it to homes, schools, and businesses.

It is getting colder and colder and the trees are getting smaller and smaller.

"I learned in Bison School that as you go farther north, the trees look like little sticks and the ground stays permanently frozen. It's called permafrost." Bou is a gold-star student.

Water and wind power are both forms of renewable energy produced in Manitoba.

No slouch herself, Mary observes, "The trees only have branches on one side. I wonder if the tricky North Wind did that."

"He did! He did!" the little stick trees call out. "He blows so hard that our branches can only grow on the south side."

Mary and Bou giggle and wave. Trees that talk!

They see the gigantic Hudson Bay stretching out in front of them.

Mary and Bou hear clicking noises. They hear squeaking noises. The noises get nearer and nearer, clearer and clearer until they see a group of bright white beluga whales playing in the water.

"Welcome to Hudson Bay!" the whales click and squeak.

Mary and Bou flit and flutter over the belugas, enjoying their funny whale talk.

Mary notices the steadily sinking sun. They wave good-bye and fly back to shore.

Between 1684 and its closing in 1957, York Factory served as the northern headquarters for the Hudson's Bay Company. The fort is located on the Hayes River, just inland from Hudson Bay.

Up ahead, something glitters in the sun's fading rays.

"It's the torch!" cries Mary. "Polar bears found it!"

"Be careful," Bou whispers. "We can't bother a mother bear with cubs."

Mary and Bou silently swirl toward the torch, but the polar bears spot them. Snarling, the mother bear swats them to the ground and lunges, sharp teeth bared.

Mary feels the bear's hot breath on her face and squeezes her eyes shut.

Wapusk National Park protects one of the world's largest known polar bear denning grounds, where bear cubs are born. "Wapusk" is the Cree word for "white bear."

Suddenly, the North Wind bursts in, carrying Mary, Bou, and the torch safely away from the grouchy bears.

"You've found the torch!" the North Wind whoops.

"Thanks for rescuing us," says Mary, "but you have some explaining to do, Mr. Wind. Why did you knock me into Lake Winnipeg?"

"Sorry," the North Wind apologizes. "I was just goofing around."

"Sheesh. Now I know how my brother feels when I tease him," mumbles Mary.

"We need to hurry," says Bou. "The sun's setting!"

Dismayed, Mary considers the drenched torch. "How will we light it?"

"Look up," says the North Wind.

The northern lights are dancing in the night sky. They whirl around the torch until the flame returns.

Another name for the northern lights is the aurora borealis, a natural light display that can sometimes be seen in the night sky in the northern hemisphere. These light displays also appear in the southern hemisphere, but are called aurora australis.

The North Wind hands Mary the torch.
"Let's get this torch back to the Golden Boy!"
Bou exclaims.
They wave good-bye to the northern lights.
The North Wind zips and zooms Mary and Bou all
the way back to Winnipeg.

A statue of Louis Riel stands near the Legislative Building. Riel was a Métis leader who played an important role in Manitoba becoming a province in 1870.

The Golden Boy is
so pleased that he dances
a jig on the dome of the
Legislative Building. He
proudly faces north again,
holding his torch and his
sheaf of wheat, the symbols
of Manitoba's strong future.
The North Wind puffs a
good-bye and disappears.

Mary pats Bou's furry head.
"I'd better go home."
"Come visit again,"
says Bou.

Mary taps her atlas – tap tap tap – and opens it to the page
where she lives. The atlas fizzles and sizzles. It splutters and
splatters. It bubbles and pops. Mary grows bigger and bigger,
taller and taller, larger and larger. In a flurry of sparks and mist,
she is back in her bedroom.

Mary hears her brother in the hallway.

"I guess I'd better go apologize," she mutters.

She spots her box of fake spiders. "Now that would be interesting."

Then Mary smiles.

Dear Readers,

There are many interesting places in Manitoba that we did not get a chance to visit. Here are just a few:

Tall Grass Prairie Preserve

Walk through the tall grasses and wildflowers on the Agassiz Interpretive Trail.

Narcisse Snake Dens

Tens of thousands of red-sided garter snakes hibernate in the underground limestone caverns. The dens are world famous for the spectacular snake activity that occurs each spring and fall.

Oak Hammock Marsh

People from all over the world come to see the hundreds of species of birds and other wildlife that hang out in this restored wetland. A bird's eye view of the marsh reveals a pond shaped like a duck swimming.

Churchill

Churchill is known as the polar bear capital of the world. You can also paddle with the belugas.

The National and Provincial Parks

Manitoba's two national parks are Riding Mountain National Park and Wapusk National Park.

Manitoba also has approximately eighty provincial parks.

Whiteshell Provincial Park has two hundred lakes for fabulous fishing, including West Hawk, the province's deepest lake.

If you like sand, visit the desert-like area of Spirit Sands in Spruce Woods Provincial Park, or enjoy Grand Beach Provincial Park, home to one of the best white sand beaches in North America.

We hope you have fun meeting Manitoba!

Your friends,

Mary & Bou